PIPER GREEN *and* *the* FAIRY TREE

PIE GIRL

Book

 5

PIPER GREEN and the FAIRY TREE

PIE GIRL

ELLEN POTTER *Illustrated by* QIN LENG

Alfred A. Knopf | Yearling
New York

Text copyright © 2017 by Ellen Potter
Jacket art and interior illustrations copyright © 2017 by Qin Leng

All rights reserved. Published in the United States by Alfred A. Knopf, an imprint of Random House Children's Books, a division of Penguin Random House LLC, New York.

All rights reserved. Published in the United States by Yearling, an imprint of Random House Children's Books, a division of Penguin Random House LLC, New York.

Knopf, Borzoi Books, and the colophon are registered trademarks of Penguin Random House LLC.

Yearling and the jumping horse design are registered trademarks of Penguin Random House LLC.

Visit us on the Web! randomhousekids.com

Educators and librarians, for a variety of teaching tools, visit us at
RHTeachersLibrarians.com

Library of Congress Cataloging-in-Publication Data
Names: Potter, Ellen, author. | Leng, Qin, illustrator.
Title: Pie Girl / Ellen Potter ; illustrated by Qin Leng.
Description: First edition. | New York : Alfred A. Knopf, 2017. | Series: Piper Green and the fairy tree ; [book 2] | "A Yearling Book." | Summary: Piper Green looks forward to serving pie at Peek-a-Boo Island's annual potluck supper, but a food allergy upsets her plan.
Identifiers: LCCN 2017021197 (print) | LCCN 2016044754 (ebook) |
ISBN 978-1-101-93968-0 (pbk.) | ISBN 978-1-101-93966-6 (lib. bdg.) |
ISBN 978-1-101-93967-3 (ebook)
Subjects: | CYAC: Community life—Maine—Fiction. | Food allergy—Fiction. | Family life—Maine—Fiction. | Islands—Fiction. | Maine—Fiction. | BISAC: JUVENILE FICTION / Family / General (see also headings under Social Issues). | JUVENILE FICTION / Imagination & Play. | JUVENILE FICTION / School & Education.
Classification: LCC PZ7.P8518 (print) | LCC PZ7.P8518 Pie 2017 (ebook) | DDC [E]—dc23

The text of this book is set in 17-point Mrs. Eaves.
The illustrations were created using ink and digital painting.

Printed in the United States of America
September 2017
10 9 8 7 6 5 4 3 2 1
First Edition

First Yearling Edition 2017

For all the wonderful people at Island Readers
& Writers and the Maine Seacoast Mission,
who bring books and joy to Pie Girls
and Potato Ploppers
—E.P.

To sweet-tooth Mark
—Q.L.

Crow Island

Egg Island

Mink Island School

MAINLAND

MINK ISLAND

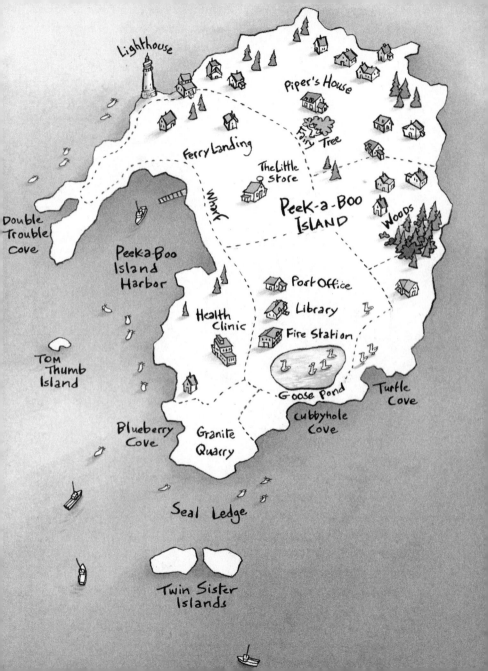

CHAPTER ONE

THE IMPORTANT STUFF

My name is Piper Green and I live on Peek-a-Boo Island.

There are two things you should know about Peek-a-Boo Island:

1. All the kids on the island ride a lobster boat to school.

2. There is a Fairy Tree in my front yard.

There's something else in my front yard too. It's my toothbrush. Last week, Mom said my toothbrush was too old and I had to throw it out. That made me very upset because my toothbrush and I have been through a lot together.

"Mom, no!" I cried. "I love that toothbrush!"

"Piper, the bristles are falling out."

"Dad's losing the bristles on his *head*," I said. "Are you going to throw him in the garbage too?"

After that, Mom said we could give my toothbrush a proper burial in our front yard. We put it in an empty spaghetti box with some toothpaste for company. At the

funeral, Mom told me I should say a few words about my toothbrush.

I thought for a minute.

"You were a good toothbrush," I said. "You always cleaned my teeth into sparkling beauties, and you didn't even mind when my breath stank." Then, very quietly, I whispered to the box, "I'll never brush my teeth again."

Mom heard me, though, and she said that would be a great idea, if I wanted to have teeth like Grandma Green.

"But Grandma Green has those clip-on teeth," I said.

"Exactly," said Mom.

CHAPTER TWO

POOF!

"Apple pie, pecan pie, butterscotch swirl,
Pumpkin pie, lumpkin pie,
I'm the pie GIRL!"

I made up that song this morning. I sang it as I walked to the Little Store with my younger brother, Leo. Every time I got to the part that went "GIRL," I did a hop.

"There's no such thing as lumpkin pie," said Leo.

Actually, I knew that. Except "lumpkin" was the only word that sounded good with "pumpkin."

I ignored him and sang my pie girl song again very loudly. I was in a joyful mood this morning, and I didn't want anything to ruin it. That's because today the *Sea Star* was coming. The *Sea Star* is a ship that sails around the coast of Maine, helping people who live on the islands. The *Sea Star*'s crew brings food when the weather is bad and people can't get across to the mainland, and at Christmas, they give all the kids presents. Plus, once a year, they bring doctors to the islands so that people can have checkups. Today they were coming with a doctor. But that's not the good part. The good part was afterward, when there would be a potluck supper on board the ship. Everyone on the island brings food to the potluck supper, and whatever dish your family makes, the kids get to serve it.

This year, Mom was making pecan pie. That made me the Pie Girl.

The Little Store was very busy this morning. It is Peek-a-Boo Island's only grocery store, and it sells all kinds of things—bread, milk, cheese, ice cream, rubber gloves for lobstermen, and lots of other stuff too. Mrs. Spratt was behind the checkout counter. Her cash register kept going *Ping! Ping! Ping!* as people bought ingredients for their dish in the potluck supper.

I looked at our list:

  2 bags of pecans
  1 bag of brown sugar
  1 bag of flour

Suddenly, I felt something *bonk* the back of my head.

"Hey!" I shouted as I turned around. Allie O'Malley was standing behind me, waving a wand with a silver glittery star on the end of it.

"What's the big idea?" I demanded, rubbing my head.

"I was poofing you," said Allie. She waved her wand around in the air. "Poof, poof! I'm being a fairy today. See? I'm wearing my brand-new fairy skirt." She twirled around to show off her skirt, which was made of green and silver cloth strips that were pointy on the bottom. It was very beautiful. Then she bonked Leo on the head with her wand.

"Poof!" she said.

"OW!" cried Leo.

"Fairies don't go around poofing people on their skulls, you know," I told her.

"Says who?" Allie O'Malley asked.

Right then I really felt like telling her about the Fairy Tree in my front yard. Except I didn't because it's a secret. The only other person who knows about the Fairy Tree is my next-door neighbor, Mrs.

Pennypocket. There is a hole inside the Fairy Tree's trunk, and if you put something in there, the fairies will take it and leave you a special gift in its place.

I shut my mouth very tightly in case the Fairy Tree secret tried to sneak out of me.

"My mom is making a deviled eggs appetizer for potluck," said Allie O'Malley as she swished her wand around. "So I'm going to be Appetizer Girl this year. Appetizer Girl is kind of like the star of the show because appetizers get served first."

"Well, I'm going to be Pie Girl," I said proudly.

Allie O'Malley frowned. "No you're not," she said. "You're Mashed Potato

Girl. Your mother always makes mashed potatoes, so you are *always* Mashed Potato Girl."

"Well, guess what? This year, Mom isn't making mashed potatoes." I put my hand on my hip and bopped it to one side, very sassy.

"I liked it better when she made mashed potatoes," Leo said.

"That's because you were Gravy Boy," I told him.

Gravy Boy gets to pour the gravy from a little ceramic ship that is shaped like the *Titanic*. Mashed Potato Girl just plops the mashed potatoes on people's plates. No one wants to be a potato plopper.

"This year our mom is making pecan pie," I said to Allie, shaking the bag of pecans at her, "so I'm going to be Pie Girl. *Pie Girl.*"

I could tell that Allie was not happy about this news. Pie Girl is definitely better than Appetizer Girl because who doesn't love pie?

Mr. Aronson walked by with a shopping basket full of stuff. Allie screeched and jumped backward, squinching up her eyes.

"What's the matter?" asked Leo.

"Salt!" Allie shrieked, pointing to the container of salt in Mr. Aronson's basket.

"So? What's wrong with salt?" I asked.

"Fairies hate salt!"

"No they don't," I told her.

"Yes they do, Piper. They hate salt and they hate the sound of bells and they love butterflies that are yellow and they love riding on giant rats."

"Says who?" I asked.

"My big fairy encyclopedia. It knows everything there is to know about fairies."

I felt a little sick in my stomach just then.

"They probably just don't like too *much* salt," I said with a nervous voice.

"Wrong!" Allie jabbed the wand at me. "Fairies hate any salt at all. My encyclopedia says that if you want to get rid of fairies, just sprinkle salt all around their house and they'll go away."

Uh-oh.

Because guess what I left for the fairies yesterday?

A pretzel rod. And that thing was covered with salt.

CHAPTER THREE

FAIRY TREASURES

Right after we brought home the groceries, I ran outside to the fat red maple tree in the front of our yard. That's the Fairy Tree. I figured I would take the salty pretzel out of the Fairy Tree, just in case Allie's encyclopedia was right.

I scrambled up the tree and then sat in the crook of two branches, beside the hole in the trunk.

"Hello in there," I said into the hole. "I'm just going to take back that pretzel

I left for you guys. I didn't know about the salt thing. I don't have a fairy encyclopedia."

I reached into the hole and felt around for the pretzel. Except there was nothing in there. No pretzel, no nothing. That was strange! When the fairies take what I leave for them, they always leave something else in its place.

I patted around in the fairy hole one more time, just to be sure. It was totally empty.

That bad feeling came back into my stomach again. Because maybe the salty pretzel had made them leave. What if the fairies were gone for good!

I climbed back down the tree and ran next door to Mrs. Pennypocket's house. Mrs. Pennypocket is an expert on the Fairy Tree, since it was her grandmother who found the Fairy Tree in the first place.

I knocked on her door.

"Come in!" Mrs. Pennypocket called from inside.

Her house smelled very delicious. I found Mrs. Pennypocket in her kitchen, bending over the open oven.

"I have a problem," I told her.

"Do you?" she said. "Well, I'd better hear about it. Sit down and make yourself comfortable while I give these baked beans a stir."

I sat down at the kitchen table. Nigel the bull terrier waddled up to me with his tail wagging. I gave his big, fat head a few pats.

Mrs. Pennypocket closed the oven door, took off her oven mitts, and sat down across from me.

"Okay, Piper," she said, folding her hands on the table. "Let's hear about your problem."

So I told her what Allie O'Malley had said about the salt, and I told her about the pretzel rod and how the fairies might have run away, all because of me. Then I started to cry. That made Nigel start crying too, only he cried in little squeaks. He put his head on my leg, and we both cried together.

"Oh dear, you two are breaking my heart," said Mrs. Pennypocket, looking at Nigel and me sadly. "Hmm. Let me ponder this." She got up and took a few oatmeal raisin cookies out of her rooster cookie jar and put them on a plate. Then she set the plate on the table and sat back down. She picked up a cookie and nibbled on it. I think it was helping her to ponder.

"Well, as best as I can remember," she finally said, "my grandmother never mentioned anything about fairies not liking salt. In fact, she said that the Fairy Tree had only one rule: you leave a treasure and you take a treasure." Mrs. Penny-pocket looked at me carefully. "Did you really treasure that pretzel, Piper?"

"Yes, I did!" I told her loudly. "I loved that pretzel."

She kept staring at me.

I looked at my hands. Then I looked up at the ceiling. Finally, I looked at Mrs. Pennypocket.

"Maybe I didn't really treasure that pretzel so much," I admitted. I scratched Nigel behind the ear. "And I might have taken a bite out of it too. It was left over from my lunch box."

"All right, then maybe you could leave something else for the fairies," Mrs.

Pennypocket suggested. "It should be something really special this time. How about something that you made? Those are always the best sorts of things."

I had to ponder that, so I took a cookie and nibbled it. I had to eat two of them before I came up with a really good idea.

"Got it!" I said, and I snapped my fingers. I'm a lousy snapper, though, so it was really just a fast rub.

I hopped out of the chair. "Thanks for the help!" I called as I headed for the door. Quick as anything, I ran back to the Fairy Tree and climbed up again.

"I'm really sorry about the pretzel," I said into the fairy hole. "I have something else for you, though. I made it myself. Ready? Okay, here it is." Then, in my nicest voice, I sang the song that I had made up that morning:

"Apple pie, pecan pie, butterscotch swirl,
Pumpkin pie, lumpkin pie,
I'm the pie GIRL!"

CHAPTER
FOUR

GRRRR!

Back in our kitchen, Mom gave me three lumps of pie dough and a rolling pin. She showed me how to put flour on the table and roll out the crust until it got bigger and bigger.

I have wanted to use a rolling pin for my whole entire life! Only now I couldn't enjoy it because I kept worrying about the fairies.

What if Mrs. Pennypocket was wrong and the fairy encyclopedia was right? Maybe the fairies really did go away. Maybe they

moved to another tree. Maybe they moved to one of *Allie O'Malley's* trees because she knew all about the salt and the giant rats.

I kept on worrying and rolling and worrying and rolling until I remembered . . . if the fairies left me something for my Pie Girl song, I'd know that they were still here!

I put the rolling pin down and ran for the door so that I could check the Fairy Tree.

"Hold on there, Speedy! Where are you going?" Mom asked. She and Leo were stirring the ingredients for the pie filling.

"I'll be back in a minute," I told her. "I just have to check on something."

"Finish rolling out the crusts first," she said.

"*Grrrr.*" I showed my teeth.

"Did you just growl at me?" Mom said. Her eyebrows were lifted up, and that means she is not in the mood for any monkey business, young lady.

I shook my head and went back to rolling out the piecrusts.

"I hope the *Sea Star* brings Dr. Dagan and not Dr. Scott," said Leo as he poured the pecans into a measuring cup. "Dr. Scott always has cold hands, and his breath smells like bananas."

Leo is an expert on doctors, since he has gone to a lot of them. That's because of his right ear, which has no hearing in it. Mom and Dad didn't even know he was deaf in that ear until he was three years old and would pick up the phone when it rang. He'd put the phone to his right ear and say, "Hello? *Hellooooo?*" and then hang up.

"Nobody's there," he'd tell my parents. Then the person would call back and wonder why Leo had hung up on them.

That's when my parents brought him to a doctor, who said Leo was totally deaf in his right ear. He doesn't wear a hearing aid because the doctors said it wouldn't help him, so you probably wouldn't even know he can't hear in one ear, except for if you try to whisper a secret into it.

Mom came over to check on my crust.

"Hmm," she said, tilting her head this way and that. "It looks a little lopsided." She pulled off a piece from one side and put it on the other. "Now roll that in, and I think it will be nice and round."

I growled again, but only in my head this time.

After I finished that crust, I had to roll out two more, which took FOREVER.

"Done!" I said, and I ran straight out the door to the Fairy Tree.

I climbed up the tree and sat down in the crook. Then I took a deep breath and closed my eyes.

"Please let there be something in there,

please let there be something in there," I
whispered. Then I reached my hand into
the fairy hole.

"Oh no, oh *noooo!*" I cried.

There was nothing in there. Not a
speck.

"The fairies really *are* gone! I ruined
everything with that dumb pretzel."

But then my fingers felt something. It
was on the bottom of the hole, so flat and
smooth that I must have missed it the first
time.

"Yay, yay, yay! You're still here, fairies!"
I shouted into the hole happily.

I pulled out the thing that they had left
for me.

It was a pirate eye patch.

"Thank you!" I hugged the Fairy Tree very tight.

Except I wasn't sure why I needed a pirate eye patch, since I was going to be a taco for Halloween. Still, Mrs. Pennypocket says that even though the Fairy Tree might not leave you something you want, it always leaves you something that you really need . . . even if you don't *know* that you need it.

I put the eye patch on right away.

"I promise I am going to wear this all day long," I told the fairies.

Then I remembered something.

Oops.

I was going to be Pie Girl today. And I have never seen a Pie Girl wearing a pirate eye patch.

CHAPTER
FIVE

PIE GIRL PIRATE

For the potluck supper, I dressed in my favorite dress. It is blue with white polka dots all over it and a black belt that is shiny. I put on my best black shoes too. When I was all dressed, I went down the hall to the bathroom to admire myself in the big mirror. Just as I got to the bathroom, Dad walked out of it. His hair was wet from a shower, and he was dressed in his nice clothes.

"You look very gorgeous," I told him.

"So do you," he said. Then he stared at my head for a second.

"What's up with the eye patch?" he asked.

"I'm wearing it to the potluck," I told him.

"Think again, pal," he told me.

I tapped the side of my head for a moment, then said, "Okay, I just thought again. And I think that I am definitely wearing this eye patch."

Dad's face looked unfriendly. Then he called for my mom.

She came to the bathroom, all dressed up in her nice yellow sweater that Grandma made for her.

"Piper says she's wearing that eye patch to the potluck," Dad told her.

Uh-oh. Now they were both frowning at my head.

"Why are you wearing that eye patch, Piper?" Mom asked. Her voice was the kind of voice that is waiting for an interesting answer.

I couldn't tell her it was because I had promised the fairies I would.

"I just feel like it," I said.

"But you're going to be Pie Girl," said Mom. "Pie Girl doesn't wear an eye patch."

"Yes, but I'm the *pirate* kind of Pie Girl," I told her.

Then Mom took a deep breath, which is how she relaxes herself when she's stressed out.

"Choose your battles, choose your battles," she muttered to Dad, patting him on the back before she walked away.

The *Sea Star* was moored at the public dock. It is a big ship with a dark green hull. Captain MacArthur was standing out on the deck to greet people.

"Well, hello, Green family! Good to see you all again!" When he spotted me, he folded his arms across his chest and blocked my way.

"Sorry, no pirates allowed aboard this ship," he said.

"But I'm a Pie Girl Pirate," I told him.

"Ah, well, that's okay, then. Do you know what pirates say when they serve pie?"

I shook my head.

"They say, 'Shiver me timbers, be ye like some pie?'" While he said this, he made a hook out of his finger, like Captain Hook.

I tried that out. "Shiver me timbers, be ye like some pie?" and I made a hook out of my finger.

"Good. Now give us a snarl."

I did a snarl.

"You'll do," said Captain MacArthur. He stepped aside. "Just keep the swash-buckling to a minimum."

There were loads of people from Peek-a-Boo Island already on the *Sea Star*. The little kids were running around like nutjobs, and bigger kids were playing games at tables while the grown-ups were talking.

I helped Mom and Dad carry the pies into the galley, which is the ship's kitchen. On the way, I sang my Pie Girl song.

> *"Apple pie, pecan pie, butterscotch swirl,*
> *Pumpkin pie, lumpkin pie,*
> *I'm the pie GIRL!"*

I even did the hop, but it was just a tiny hop because I was holding one of the pies.

The counters in the galley were packed with food. But bad luck, because guess who was also there? Allie O'Malley and her mother. Allie O'Malley was still wearing her fairy dress and her hair was in a French braid. She and her mother were fussing over a silver tray full of deviled eggs. The hard-boiled eggs were cut in half, and the yellow filling was made to look like a baby chick peeping out. Each little chick had a sliver of carrot for a beak and two black peppercorn eyes. They were very adorable.

I took the foil off of one of our pecan pies. The pecans were all messy. They didn't look like anything.

Some of the pecans were poking up, so I pushed them down with my finger. Then I saw two that were overlapping, so I took one out. But that made a hole in the pie. I did some more rearranging until Mom said, "Jeezum crow, Piper! Hands off the pie!"

Allie O'Malley looked over at us. Then she looked at the pie and made a little sniff sound.

I did a pirate snarl at her. It was an excellent one too, but she just rolled her eyes.

CHAPTER
SIX

CHECKUP

"Piper!" Camilla called to me.

My friends Camilla and Jacob were sitting at one of the tables, playing a game of Jenga. Camilla was talking a mile a minute because that girl is a motormouth. When she saw me, she said, "Guess what? The doctor said I'm probably going to be tall when I grow up, and that's good because I'm thinking about becoming a storm chaser and if I have long legs I can run faster to catch up with the storms. Oh, and you know what else? I just used the bathroom downstairs because the one in the nurse's station is broken and guess what? They have candy-cane hand soap down there! Plus, when you flush the toilet it is soooo loud! And you know what else? My cousin just got a GINORMOUS lizard named Mr. Biscuit . . ."

As Camilla was yakking, Jacob was carefully looking at the Jenga tower. He's an expert Jenga player. I've never even beaten that guy once.

"Your turn," said Jacob after he pushed out his block.

Camilla just kept on talking while she quickly poked her finger at a block and took it out of the tower. The tower swayed and I squeezed up my eyes, ready for it to fall, but it didn't. Jacob put his chin in his hand and looked at the tower again. Then he pushed out a block near the bottom very, very slowly.

RAKA-CRACKA-CRACKA!!!

The Jenga blocks fell all over the place.

Jacob threw up his hands and shook his head. "I don't get it. That's the third time she's beaten me today. She doesn't even *look* at what she's doing, she's so busy talking."

"I think with my mouth," Camilla said, shrugging.

A nurse stepped out of the doctor's cabin toward the bow of the ship and called, "Piper and Leo?"

"Good luck, Piper!" Camilla said as I got up to go to the doctor's cabin with Mom and Leo. "I hope you're going to be tall too. Then we can both chase storms!"

When we walked into the cabin, Dr. Dagan looked at Leo and me with a frown.

"I think there's been some mistake," she said. "Piper and Leo Green were supposed to be next, and they are *much* smaller than the two of you. Can you go back out there and tell Piper and Leo to come in?"

Mom smiled, so I knew Dr. Dagan was just joking around, but Leo said, "We *are* Piper and Leo! We just grew since you last saw us. If you want proof, look!" He held up Michelle.

Michelle is a piece of paper.

"Ah, now I *do* recognize your friend Michelle!" Dr. Dagan said.

"She's his wife now," I told Dr. Dagan.

Leo looked very proud of himself.

"Congratulations, Leo," said Dr. Dagan.

"And that's Harold, our son." He pointed to the yellow Post-it note clipped onto Michelle. A few weeks ago, Harold's sticky back got some cat hair on it, and it doesn't stick anymore, so now Leo attaches him to Michelle with a binder clip.

"Harold is very handsome. Should I examine him first?" Dr. Dagan patted the metal table that was covered with a long piece of waxy paper.

Leo loved that idea. He unclipped Harold and put him on the metal table.

Dr. Dagan stuck her stethoscope in her ears and put the other end on Harold. She listened for a minute. Then she said, "His heartbeat is nice and strong."

"He doesn't actually have a heart, Dr. Dagan," Leo said. "He's too flat."

"Oh, you're right. Sorry." Dr. Dagan tapped Harold in a few places and shined her flashlight on him.

"His complexion is good. He's a lovely shade of yellow," said Dr. Dagan.

"Don't worry about that smudge there." Leo pointed to a pink spot on Harold. "It's just some old spaghetti sauce I splattered on him."

"Well," Dr. Dagan said, "I think Harold is in excellent health."

Carefully, she clipped Harold back on Michelle.

Next was Leo's turn. Mom held Michelle

while Leo stepped onto the scale and Dr. Dagan checked his height and weight. Then she told him to hop up on the table. Dr. Dagan put the blood pressure cuff on him. While it strangled his arm, Dr. Dagan asked Leo about his good ear. She never asks about his bad ear because Leo goes to a special ear doctor for that. Next she asked him a bunch of questions, like how much exercise he gets and if he eats vegetables. He told her he eats them, but I happen to know he sticks them down his pants when Mom and Dad aren't looking.

Pretty soon it was my turn. Dr. Dagan weighed me and measured me too. She didn't say I was going to be tall like

Camilla, so I don't know about that storm-chasing thing. After she put that arm strangler on me, Dr. Dagan pulled out her little silver flashlight with the bird's beak on the tip. She stuck that thing right up my nose to have a look around. Nothing interesting ever happens up there, but doctors always want to see for themselves.

"Do you know why pirates wore eye patches, Piper?" Dr. Dagan asked as she looked up my nose.

"Because they were missing an eyeball?" I said.

Dr. Dagan took the light out of my nose hole and put it up my other nose hole.

"Nope. They wore an eye patch because they needed one eye to always be adjusted to the dark. Imagine if you were a pirate and you suddenly had to fight in a dark place, like the lower deck. It takes a few minutes for your eyes to adjust to the dark, and that would be dangerous if someone were swinging a sword at you. But if you were wearing an eye patch, the eye under the patch would already be adjusted to the dark. All you'd have to do is switch the eye patch to your other eye, and you would be able to see." She took the light out of my nose and said, "You're not planning on taking over the *Sea Star*, are you?"

"No. I'm just being the pirate kind of

Pie Girl." Then I did my excellent snarl and said, "Shiver me timbers, be ye like some pie?" while I made a hook out of my finger.

"Hmm." Dr. Dagan frowned at my finger. "What's that?" she asked.

"A hook," I said.

"No, I mean the bumps." She held my hand and looked at it carefully.

"What is it?" Mom asked, and came over to have a look too. There were little red bumps on my finger and the palm of my hand and even a few on my wrist.

"They look like hives," Mom said.

"They do," Dr. Dagan agreed. "Piper, when did you first see these bumps?"

"Two seconds ago, when you said 'What's that?'" I told her.

The bumps were starting to feel itchy.

Dr. Dagan asked me a lot of questions then, like what I had eaten today and all the things I had done. I told her about shopping at the Little Store and rolling out all those crusts for the pecan pies. I'd had a very busy day, I realized.

"Has Piper ever eaten pecans before?" Dr. Dagan asked Mom.

Mom thought about that for a second. "Actually, I don't think she has. She didn't taste the pie today either. Although . . . she did touch it."

"I just moved some of the pecans around so they didn't look so messy."

"Well, Piper," Dr. Dagan said, folding her arms across her chest, "I suspect that you're allergic to pecans."

Allergic? But I'd never had any allergies before. Camilla has loads of allergies. She is allergic to cats, horses, hamsters, guinea pigs, dust, and flowers. Also rabbits. We had to get rid of our class rabbit, Nacho, because she is allergic to him, which means she can't be around him.

Then a horrible thought came into my brain.

"But how can I be Pie Girl if I can't be around pecan pie?" I asked Dr. Dagan.

Dr. Dagan looked at Mom.

Mom looked back at her.

I knew that look. It's the look that says, "Get ready for bad news, Piper!"

CHAPTER SEVEN

BAD NEWS

"It's not fair, it's not fair, it's NOT FAIR!"
I said after Mom and Dr. Dagan told me
I couldn't be Pie Girl. "I was supposed to
be Pie Girl! I've got the song and everything!"

"I know it's not fair," said Mom. "But
allergies are serious, Piper. It would be
hard to serve pie without some of it getting on your fingers. Next year we'll make
a blueberry pie, I promise. This year, you
can help Mrs. Grindle and Leo with the
bread."

That made things even worse.

Because being Bread Girl is a bunch of stinky fish paste.

I sat on that doctor's table and cried. Everyone was watching me, so I pulled the waxy table paper over my head to hide myself. I kept crying and crying until my eye patch felt slimy.

Someone knocked on the paper.

"What?" I said.

Leo peeped underneath.

"Can I come in?" he asked.

I sniffed. "All right."

I lifted up the paper, and Leo put his head under there with mine. He put Harold on my lap.

"Harold says he's sorry," said Leo. "He says you would have been the best Pie Girl Pirate they ever had."

I looked down at Harold with my one flooded eye.

"Thank you," I whispered to him.

My nose started to leak, but I wiped at the leak before it fell on Harold. That guy has enough problems with his spaghetti sauce splatter and his cat fur.

CHAPTER
EIGHT

STINKY FISH PASTE
BREAD GIRL

When we came out of the doctor's cabin, people were already sitting down for supper. The two long tables looked very nice. There were bright yellow tablecloths on them and centerpieces of pinecones in mason jars, with red ribbon tied around the jars. I mopped up my eyeball so people wouldn't know I was crying, although I think Jacob might have seen, and I sat down at the table, next to Dad.

"Why so gloomy?" Dad asked me.

"She's allergic to pecans," Mom told him.

"Oh?" he said. Then he cried, "Oh!" when he realized that meant no Pie Girl for me. He put his arm around me, which usually makes me feel better, but this time it didn't help at all.

Dad's younger brother, Uncle Mack, sat down across from us. He has blond hair that goes down to his shoulders, and even though he's younger than Dad, he's a lot bigger. He is Dad's sternman, which means that he helps out on Dad's lobster boat. But that's only temporary because he's saving up to get his own lobster boat, and that is all he talks about these days.

"So I went to have a look at a boat over in Rockport the other day," he said the moment he sat down. "Ooh, she was wicked sharp, I'm telling you."

Whenever Uncle Mack thinks something is great, he calls it "wicked sharp." Only he says it like this: "Wicked shaaap!"

Uncle Mack put his big arm around the chair next to him, even though the chair was empty.

"Saving that seat for some lucky girl?" Dad asked with a smile on his face.

"Any girl who sits next to me is lucky," Uncle Mack said.

It turned out the lucky girl who sat next to Uncle Mack was Nora Bean. But she didn't seem to know she was lucky because when she walked onto the *Sea Star,* Uncle Mack had to stand up and wave at her. Then he kept pointing at the empty seat until she finally sat down next to him.

It was time to give out the bread, so Leo and I each took a basket full of rolls and corn bread from Mrs. Grindle. I took my basket over to the long table on the starboard side. "Starboard" means "the right side of the ship." Leo went to the table on the port side, which is the left side of the ship.

Bread Girl is a very boring job because you just hold the basket by people's heads and they take a piece out for themselves.

Some people didn't even want bread at all since there were so many other, more exciting things to eat.

Allie O'Malley came up to the table with her tray of adorable baby-chick deviled eggs. People at the table said *"Awww!"* like they were real, actual baby chicks. Every

single person took one of those adorable things off Allie's tray.

"How come you're *Bread* Girl?" Allie O'Malley asked me. She said "Bread" just like it was stinky fish paste. "You told me you were going to be Pie Girl."

I felt my face get a little crumply with sadness again. Allie just stood there staring at me and waiting for me to answer.

"Well? Cat got your tongue, Piper?" she said in her snippety grandma voice.

My eyes started to feel hot, and they were filling up with tears.

"I'd like some bread!" someone shouted from way down the other side of the table.

I looked over. It was Jacob, which was

a very surprising thing because that boy hardly ever shouts.

I turned my back on Allie and hurried down to the other end of the table. Jacob took a piece of corn bread. Then he looked over at Allie O'Malley, who was still staring at us, and he also took two rolls.

When I finished bringing bread to everyone, I sat back down at the table. I took a peek over at Jacob. He was munching on a piece of corn bread.

And guess what else?

He was the only one at the table who didn't have one of Allie's baby chicks on his plate.

That boy is wicked shaaap.

CHAPTER
NINE

PHOOOOSH!

There was a lot of delicious food at the potluck. Mr. Aronson brought clam chowder, and Mrs. Spratt brought meatballs. Mrs. Pennypocket brought her baked beans, and the ship's steward, Gillian, made Hawaiian chicken. Camilla's family made mac and cheese, and Jacob and his dad made lobster stew. Everybody was so busy munching that no one talked. All you could hear was slurping and chomping and everyone enjoying their food. Except for me. I couldn't enjoy any of it because I just kept thinking about how it was going to break my heart to watch that pie being served without me.

After everyone had finished eating, Mom put her napkin on her plate and stood up. I knew exactly where she was going. She was getting ready to cut up the pies. Dad caught me peeking at the pies on the counter.

"Piper, you know you won't be able to eat the pecan pie, right?" he said.

"I know."

I felt my face starting to crumple up again.

"I made some fudge, Piper," said Nora Bean.

I nodded, but I didn't say anything because if I did I was going to start bawling like a big boo-hooing baby and then Allie O'Malley would see.

"I made three different kinds," Nora Bean said. "I made cookie-dough fudge and candy-cane fudge, and coconut fudge."

Oh.

That candy-cane fudge gave me an idea because it reminded me of the candy-cane bathroom soap.

I popped up out of my chair.

"Where are you going?" Dad asked.

"Bathroom." I quick ran past the galley to the stairs. At the bottom of the stairs, there was another door, and when I opened that, I was in the lower deck.

I had never been in the *Sea Star*'s lower deck before. The ship's engine sounded very loud down here. There were lots of cabins, so I walked down the hall until I saw one that had "HEAD" painted on it in big red letters. "Head" is what you call a ship's bathroom. I ducked inside and locked the door.

Now I can just hide out here until after Mom serves the pie, I thought. *That way I won't have to watch the whole tragedy with my own eyes, and no one can see me crying, especially Allie O'Malley.*

I tried to keep myself busy. First I looked in the mirror and did a snarl. But

that made me feel crummy all over again because it reminded me that I wasn't going to be able to say, "Shiver me timbers, be ye like some pie?"

I spotted the candy-cane hand soap that Camilla had told me about. The bottle was even striped red and white. I squirted some of the soap in my hand and sniffed it. It smelled exactly like a candy cane. I washed my hands with it a few times, and then I licked my hands, but they didn't taste very good.

After that, there wasn't much to do except listen to the ship's engine rumbling.

Suddenly, the door latch jiggled. After that, there was a knock.

"I'm in here!" I called out.

"It's an emergency!" a voice yelled back.

I knew that voice. It was Allie O'Malley. She has about twenty emergencies every day in school.

But if I came out now, Mom would probably still be serving that pie.

"I'm not done yet!" I called.

"Is that you, Piper?" Allie said.

I just ignored her. I wasted some more time by seeing how long I could hold my breath. It turned out not very long. Then I made up a joke. Here it is: what do you get when you cross a monkey with a tornado?

A dizzy monkey.

That made me laugh out loud.

Allie pounded on the door very hard.

"I hear you laughing in there, Piper Green! You'd better let me in or I am going to have an accident and it will be your fault!" Allie shouted.

"I'm almost done!" I called back.

I flushed the toilet to make it more realistic. It didn't flush with a regular handle. You had to flush it by pressing a red button just above the toilet seat.

PHOOOOOOOOOSH!!!

Boy, Camilla was not even kidding! That thing sounded like a twelve-foot giant was drinking a Slurpee through a tiny straw!

I flushed it again.

PHOOOOOOOOOSH!!!

And again.

PHOOOOOOOOOSH!!!

It was when I flushed it the third time that the ship's engine stopped rumbling and the lights went out.

CHAPTER
TEN

SPOOOOOKY!

"Oh no, *oh no!*" I squeaked. "I broke the ship!"

It must have been the third flush that did it.

"Why are all the lights off?" screamed Allie O'Malley from the other side of the door. "What's going on?"

I wondered if I should just keep hiding right there in the bathroom because Captain MacArthur was going to be mad when he discovered that it was me who broke his ship.

But then I realized that the toilet was "the scene of the crime," so I felt around in the dark for the door latch and I let myself out.

The hallway was so black I could hardly even see Allie, but I sure could hear her because she was screeching, "Turn on the lights, turn on the lights!"

"I can't," I told her. "I think the ship is broken."

Allie got real quiet. After a moment, she whispered, "I'm afraid of the dark."

I'm afraid of the dark too. But it's not as scary if someone else is more terrified than you are.

"It's okay, Allie. We'll just go back upstairs. I'll go first."

I put my arms in front of me and started walking. Allie grabbed the back of my dress to hold on to me. I walked very, very slowly and patted the wall until I felt a metal door. I pulled on the handle until the door opened.

"Where are we?" asked Allie.

"I'm not sure," I said as we walked through the door.

It was so dark, I couldn't see if the stairs were there. I couldn't tell where the door was either, so I wandered around, trying to find my way out. Allie held on to my dress.

"Oooooh, I don't like this," she said with a panicky voice. She sounded like she might be about to cry.

Suddenly, I had a brainchild. That's when a smart idea pops out of your brain. I remembered what Dr. Dagan had told me about how pirates wore eye patches to keep one eye adjusted to the dark. I quick switched the pirate patch to my other eye, and guess what? That Dr. Dagan actually knew what she was talking about. I really *could* see! It was shadowy, but I could tell what things were.

"It's okay, Allie, because I can see in the dark now," I told her.

"That's not funny, Piper Green," she said angrily.

"But it's true. I can see with my pirate eyeball." I looked around. "This cabin has shelves full of cans and jars," I told her to prove that I could see. "And over here is a refrigerator with a latch on it. Probably so it won't open if the ship gets tippy." I flipped the latch and opened the fridge. Even though the little fridge light didn't come on, I could still see everything inside of it. "There's milk and butter and whipped cream and eggs and packages of cheese."

Allie was quiet for a minute. Then she said, "Do you think you can get us back upstairs?"

"Yup," I said, very sure of myself. "Take my hand."

Allie held my hand, and I led the way

out of that cabin and back down the hall-way. We walked past two doors. When we got to the third door, I stopped and opened it.

"Wait. How do you know this is the right way?" Allie asked.

"Because I'm a pirate, ain't I?!" I said in my best pirate voice.

Also, the word "STAIRS" was painted on the door.

We had to go up the stairs very slowly since Allie couldn't see them and I had to tell her when to step up. We were almost to the top when someone shined a flash-light down on us.

Uh-oh.

Because the guy holding the flashlight was Captain MacArthur.

"Hi, Captain," I said.

"Piper? Allie? What are you two doing down there?" he asked.

"Um. I think the ship got broken," I said nervously. "It might have something to do with the toilet."

"The toilet?" He laughed. "No, it's just the generator. I'm going down to have a look in the engine room. Are you two okay? It's pitch-black down there. How did you find your way upstairs?"

"Because Piper has a pirate eyeball!" said Allie excitedly. "She didn't need a flashlight or anything. She can actually *see in the dark*! It was totally amazing!"

I was shocked because that girl never has anything good to say about me.

Even though Captain MacArthur was shining the flashlight for us, Allie didn't let go of my hand until we got to the top of the stairs.

I guess she's just the kind of person who is nicer in the dark.

CHAPTER
ELEVEN

PIGS AND HEARTS

It only took a few minutes for Captain MacArthur to get the power back on again. Everyone clapped. The power must have gone out right before Mom served the pie because there were plates of sliced pecan pie lined up on the galley's counter. I looked at all those slices of pie, but instead of feeling tragic, I had another brainchild. A really good one.

First I went to the ship's steward, Gillian, and asked if I could use something from the fridge downstairs. "I saw

it when Allie and I were down there in the dark."

"Of course," she said.

I ran down the stairs, and in a minute, I came back up again. Standing in front of the room, I made my finger into a hook, and with the other hand, I held up a can of whipped cream. Then I called out, "Excuse me, everybody, I have something to say!"

People stopped talking and looked at me. In my best pirate voice, I asked, "Shiver me timbers, be ye like some whipped cream with yer pie?"

Almost everyone did!

Mom served her pie, and I squirted whipped cream on each slice. I was very careful not to touch the pie with my fingers, of course. And the best part was I could make all kinds of shapes with the whipped cream. I made everyone a special shape that was just for them.

"Give me a cat," said Isabelle, one of the nutjob little kids.

"I want a turtle," said her brother, Sam.

I made a smiling face for Mr. Aronson because he has a nice big smile. "Well, look at that!" Mr. Aronson said, and he smiled that nice smile and it matched his pie face exactly.

I made Jacob a heart. That's because I'm going to marry him someday.

I made his dad a lobster, and I made Mrs. Pennypocket a tree. It looked like the Fairy Tree, and she gave me a secret wink. I made Nora Bean a pig because she has a pig named Mrs. Snortingham.

For Uncle Mack, I made a lobster boat.

Well, it looked a little bit like a hot dog wearing a hat, but Uncle Mack guessed what it was anyhow.

When I was finished, Mom and I watched everyone talking and laughing as they dug into their piece of pie.

"Nice job, Captain Hook. I'm wicked

proud of you." Mom kissed the top of my head. "Looks like you're Pie Girl after all."

"I'm something even better than Pie Girl," I said.

"You are?" Mom said.

"Yup. I'm Whipped Cream Girl!"

CHAPTER
TWELVE

WHIPPED CREAM GIRL

The next day, Mom and I made another pie. This was a pie that I could actually eat.

When it was done, Mom took a tasting bite.

"Mmm!" she said. It was a real *"Mmm"* too, not just the kind that is being polite. "Who would have thought this would be so delicious?"

Then Leo, Dad, and I all took tasting bites and we all said *"Mmm"* and we all really meant it.

"Can I take a couple of slices over to Mrs. Pennypocket?" I asked Mom.

"Of course." She cut two fat slices and put them on a plate. I carried the plate across the yard, but when I got to the Fairy Tree, I stopped. I put the plate down on the ground and picked up one slice of pie. Very carefully, I climbed the Fairy Tree and settled into the crook.

"Hi, fairies," I said into the hole in the trunk. "It's me, Piper. Thanks again for the pirate eye patch. If I didn't have the eye patch, I never would have had a pirate eyeball. And if I didn't have a pirate eyeball, I never would have been Whipped Cream Girl. And guess what?

Captain MacArthur said I was the hit of the party." I held the pie up to the fairy hole. "I brought something for you guys. It's a kind of pie you've never had before. I know because I invented it. It's called lumpkin pie. It's pumpkin pie with lumps of Marshmallow Fluff on top."

I put the lumpkin pie in the fairy hole.

"Also, I made up a new song. I think you're really going to like it. Ready? Okay, here it is . . .

"Whipped cream, whupped cream, pile it high.
Perfect on pudding,
Better on pie.
Squiggle it, sploosh it, make a big swirl.
Hunka munka, Whipped Cream Girl!"

THE END

ABOUT THE AUTHOR

Although she doesn't ride a lobster boat to work, **Ellen Potter** can look out her window and see islands, just like the one Piper lives on. Ellen is the author of many books for children, including the award-winning Olivia Kidney series. She lives in Maine with her family and an assortment of badly behaved creatures. Learn more about Ellen at ellenpotter.com.

ABOUT THE ILLUSTRATOR

Qin Leng was born in Shanghai and lived in France and Montreal, where she studied at the Mel Hoppenheim School of Cinema. She has received many awards for her animated short films and artwork, and has published numerous picture books. Qin currently lives and works as a designer and illustrator in Toronto.

Life on an island in Maine is always interesting.
Then Piper Green discovers a Fairy Tree in her front yard.
Is the Fairy Tree really magic?
And can it fix her problems?

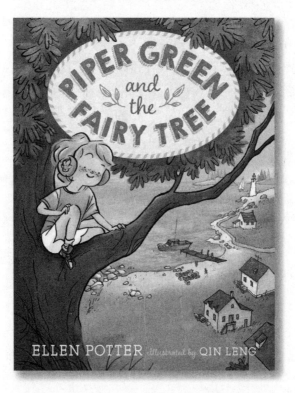

Piper Green's day started out lucky.
But her friend says too much good luck can sometimes
turn to *bad* luck. Will the Fairy Tree in Piper's front yard
break her unlucky streak?

Piper Green just found a funny-looking whistle
hidden inside the Fairy Tree.
But what could it mean?

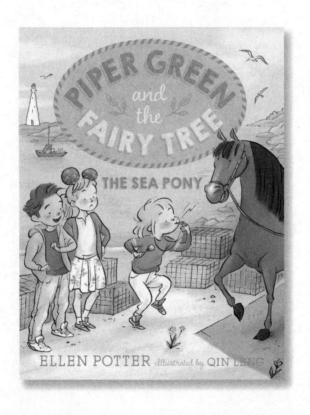

Piper Green's class is taking a pretend trip to China.
Suitcase? Check. Passport? Check.
Magic X-ray vision glasses from the Fairy Tree?
Check, check, check!